ONCE: A LULLABY

Pictures by
ANITA LOBEL

Words by bp Nichol

GREENWILLOW BOOKS • New York

Library of Congress Cataloging in Publication Data
Nichol, B. P., (date)   Once, a lullaby.
Summary: Rhymed text and illustrations describe young animals
and children in the moments just before they fall asleep.
[1. Lullabies] 1. Lobel, Anita, ill. II. Title.
PZ8.3.N5240n 1986   811'.54   85-9942
ISBN 0-688-04284-8   ISBN 0-688-04285-6 (lib. bdg.)

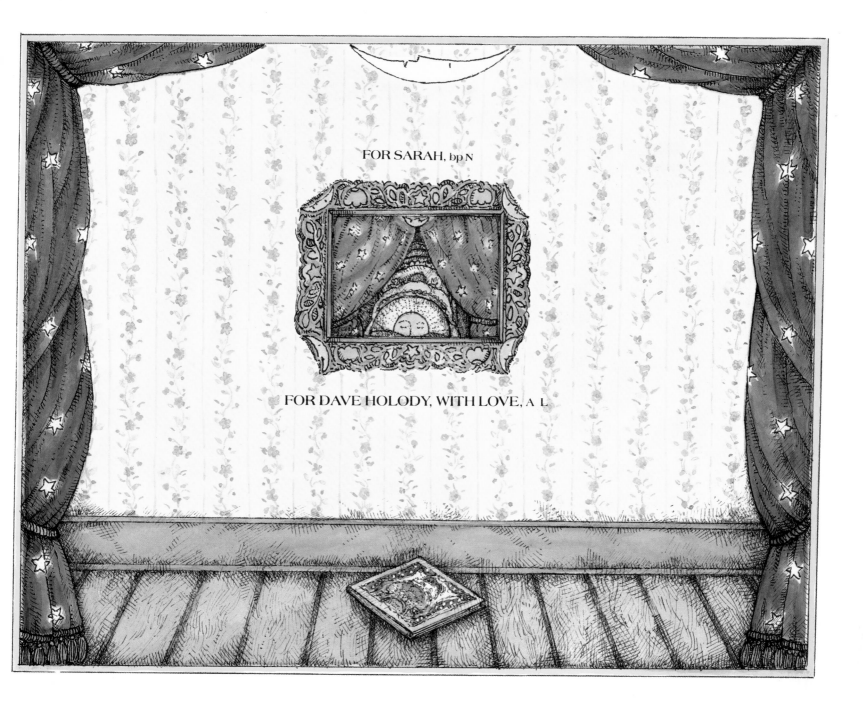

FOR SARAH, bp N

FOR DAVE HOLODY, WITH LOVE, A L

Once I was a little horse,
baby horse, little horse.
Once I was a little horse.
NEIGH, I fell asleep.

Once I was a little cow,
baby cow, little cow.
Once I was a little cow.
MOO, I fell asleep.

Once I was a little goat,
baby goat, little goat.
Once I was little goat.
MAA, I fell asleep.

Once I was a little sheep,
baby sheep, little sheep.
Once I was a little sheep.
BAA, I fell asleep.

Once I was a little pig,
baby pig, little pig.
Once I was a little pig.
OINK, I fell asleep.

Once I was a little dog,
baby dog, little dog.
Once I was a little dog.
ARF, I fell asleep.

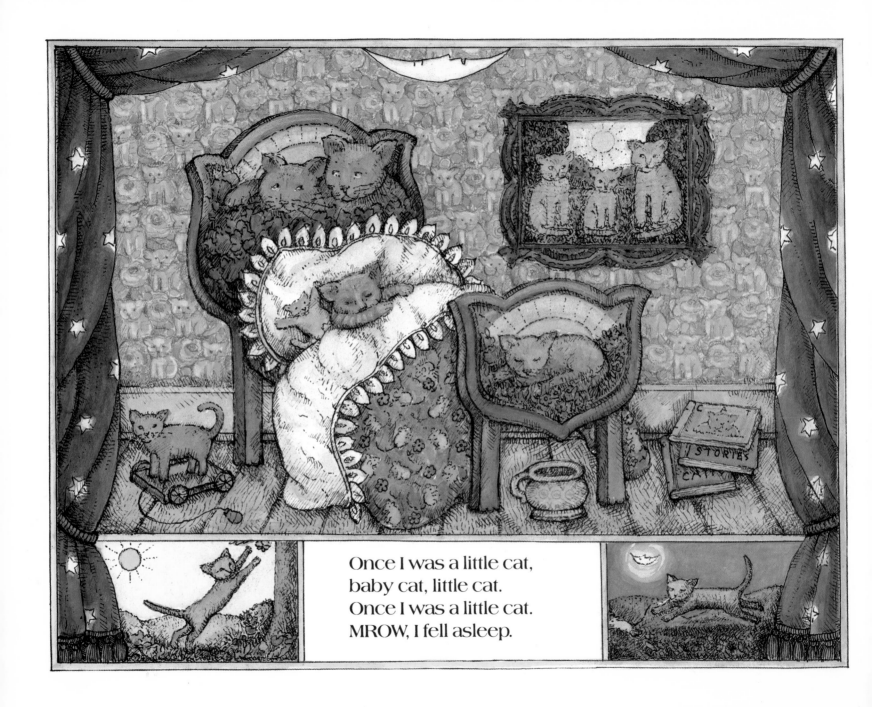

Once I was a little cat,
baby cat, little cat.
Once I was a little cat.
MROW, I fell asleep.

Once I was a little mouse,
baby mouse, little mouse.
Once I was a little mouse.
SQUEEK, I fell asleep.

Once I was a little owl,
baby owl, little owl.
Once I was a little owl.
WHOO, I fell asleep.

Once I was a little crow,
baby crow, little crow.
Once I was a little crow.
CAW, I fell asleep.

Once I was a little duck,
baby duck, little duck.
Once I was a little duck.
QUACK, I fell asleep.

Once I was a little chick,
baby chick, little chick.
Once I was a little chick.
CHEEP, I fell asleep.

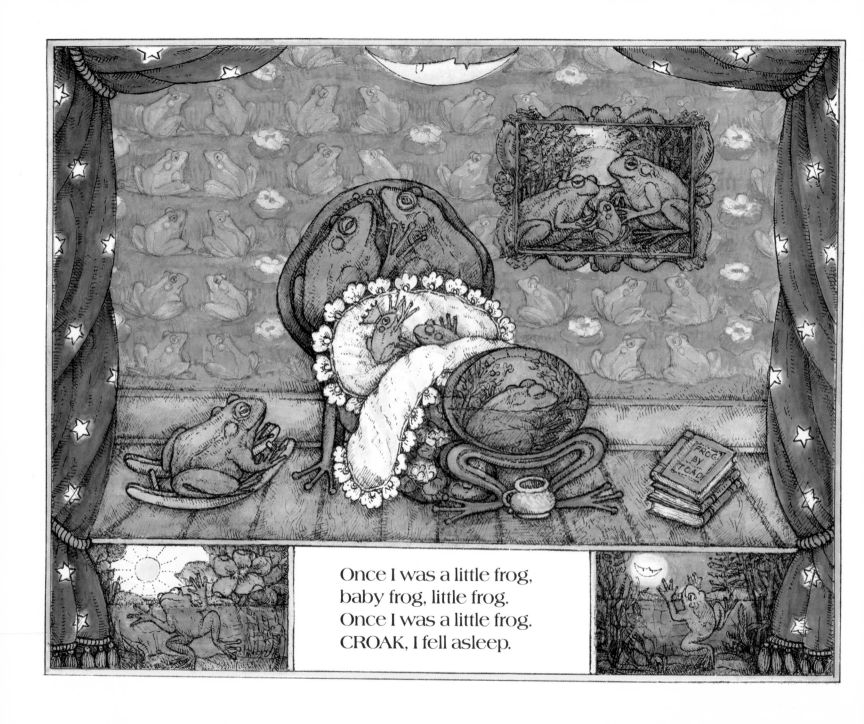

Once I was a little frog,
baby frog, little frog.
Once I was a little frog.
CROAK, I fell asleep.

Once I was a little fish,
baby fish, little fish.
Once I was a little fish.
GLUB, I fell asleep.

Once I was a little bee,
baby bee, little bee.
Once I was a little bee.
BZZZ, I fell asleep.

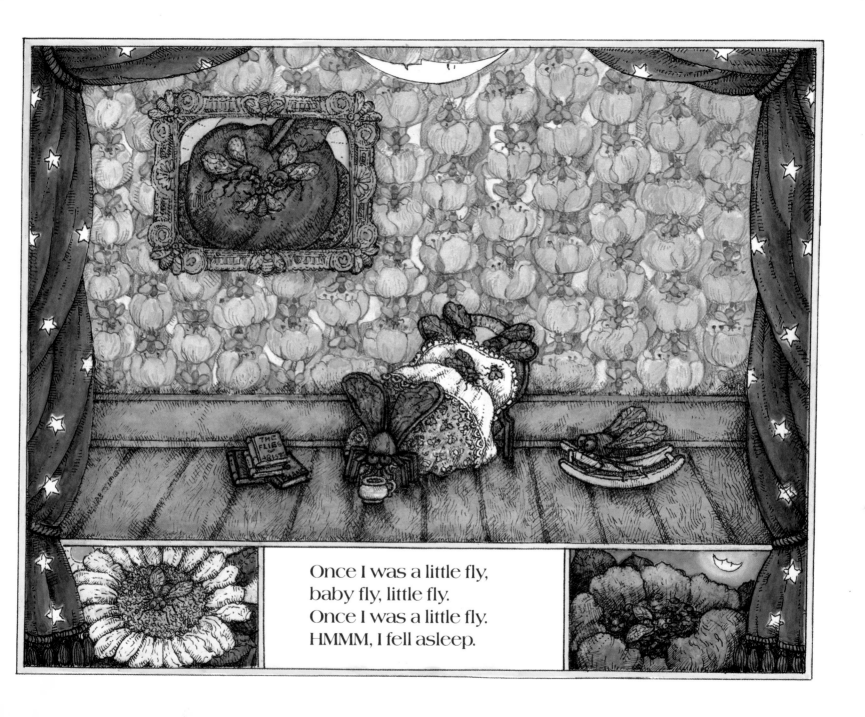

Once I was a little fly,
baby fly, little fly.
Once I was a little fly.
HMMM, I fell asleep.

Once I was a little boy,
baby boy, little boy.
Once I was a little boy.
WAA, I fell asleep.

Once I was a little girl,
baby girl, little girl.
Once I was a little girl.
WAA, I fell asleep.

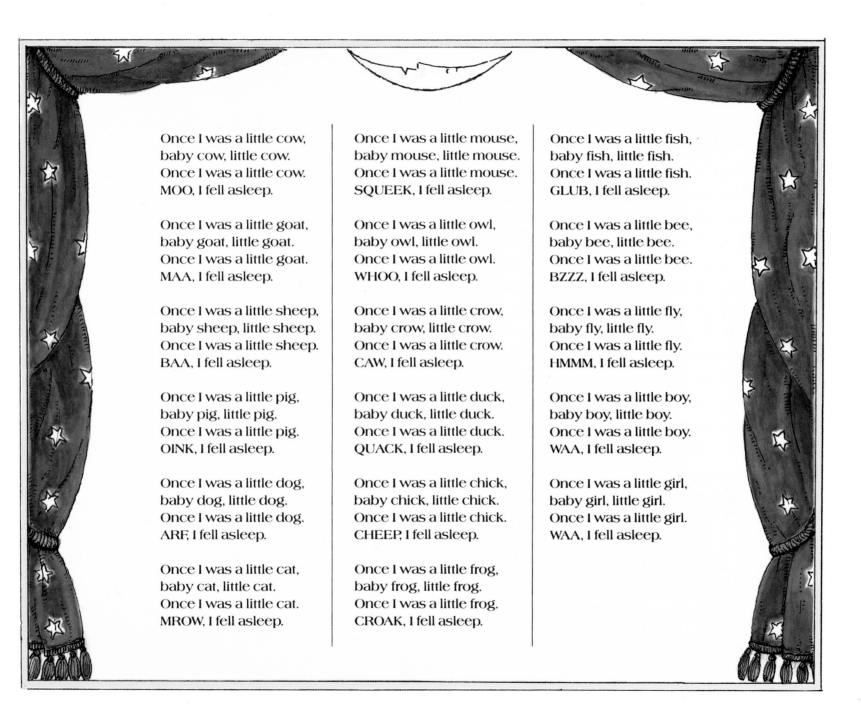

Once I was a little cow,
baby cow, little cow.
Once I was a little cow.
MOO, I fell asleep.

Once I was a little goat,
baby goat, little goat.
Once I was a little goat.
MAA, I fell asleep.

Once I was a little sheep,
baby sheep, little sheep.
Once I was a little sheep.
BAA, I fell asleep.

Once I was a little pig,
baby pig, little pig.
Once I was a little pig.
OINK, I fell asleep.

Once I was a little dog,
baby dog, little dog.
Once I was a little dog.
ARF, I fell asleep.

Once I was a little cat,
baby cat, little cat.
Once I was a little cat.
MROW, I fell asleep.

Once I was a little mouse,
baby mouse, little mouse.
Once I was a little mouse.
SQUEEK, I fell asleep.

Once I was a little owl,
baby owl, little owl.
Once I was a little owl.
WHOO, I fell asleep.

Once I was a little crow,
baby crow, little crow.
Once I was a little crow.
CAW, I fell asleep.

Once I was a little duck,
baby duck, little duck.
Once I was a little duck.
QUACK, I fell asleep.

Once I was a little chick,
baby chick, little chick.
Once I was a little chick.
CHEEP, I fell asleep.

Once I was a little frog,
baby frog, little frog.
Once I was a little frog.
CROAK, I fell asleep.

Once I was a little fish,
baby fish, little fish.
Once I was a little fish.
GLUB, I fell asleep.

Once I was a little bee,
baby bee, little bee.
Once I was a little bee.
BZZZ, I fell asleep.

Once I was a little fly,
baby fly, little fly.
Once I was a little fly.
HMMM, I fell asleep.

Once I was a little boy,
baby boy, little boy.
Once I was a little boy.
WAA, I fell asleep.

Once I was a little girl,
baby girl, little girl.
Once I was a little girl.
WAA, I fell asleep.